A My Name Is...

Alice Lyne

illustrated by

Lynne Cravath

Whispering Coyote Press
BOSTON

Published by Whispering Coyote Press
480 Newbury Street, Suite 104, Danvers, MA 01923
Copyright © 1997 by Alice Lyne
Illustrations copyright © 1997 by Lynne Cravath

Printed in Hong Kong by South China Printing Company(1988) Ltd.
10 9 8 7 6 5 4 3 2 1

Book design and production by Our House
Text was set in 16-point Kabel Bold

Library of Congress Cataloging–in–Publication Data
Lyne, Alice. 1953-
A, my name is... / written by Alice Lyne; illustrated by Lynne Woodcock Cravath.
p.   cm.
Summary: A jump rope rhyme that travels through the alphabet, from Alex selling alligators in Alabama to Zelma selling zippers in Zimbabwe.
ISBN 1-879085-40-2(hardcover).   ISBN 1-879085-41-0(pbk.)
1. English language—Alphabet—Juvenile literature.   [1. Jump rope rhymes.
2. Alphabet.]   I. Cravath, Lynne Woodcock, ill.   II. Title.
PE1155.L96   1997
428.1E—dc20   96-29262
                                      CIP
                                      AC

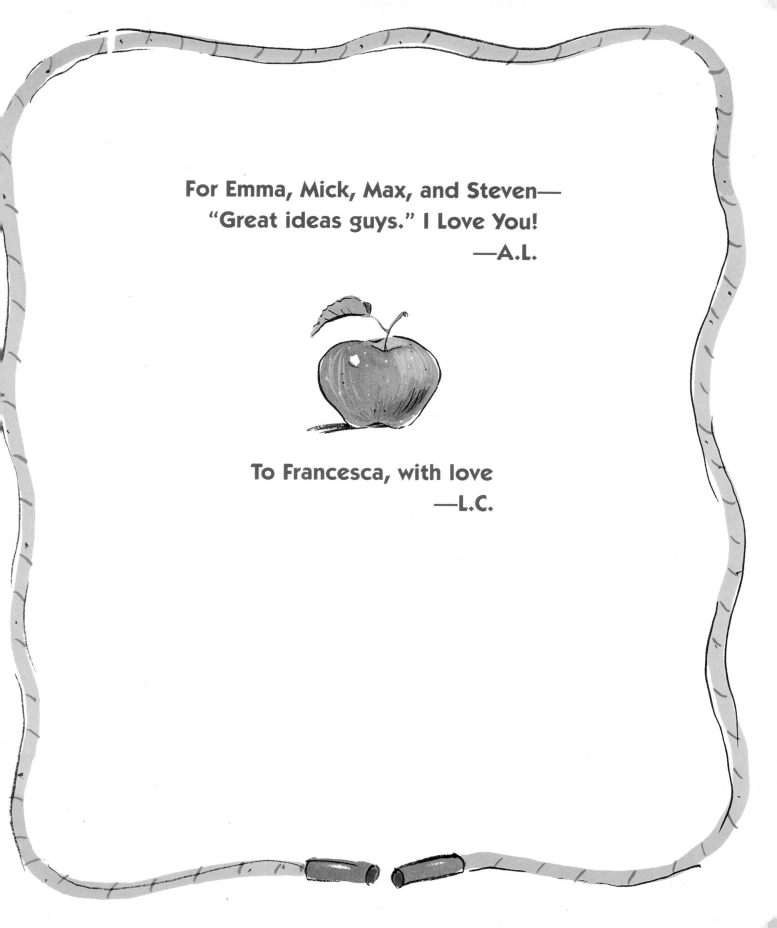

For Emma, Mick, Max, and Steven—
"Great ideas guys." I Love You!
—A.L.

To Francesca, with love
—L.C.

A a

My name is Alex,
My best friend's name is Angie,
We live in Alabama,
And we sell alligators.

My name is Becca,
My best friend's name is Billy,
We live in California,
And we sell coconuts.

My name is David,
My best friend's name is Daniel,
We live in Damascus,
And we sell diamonds.

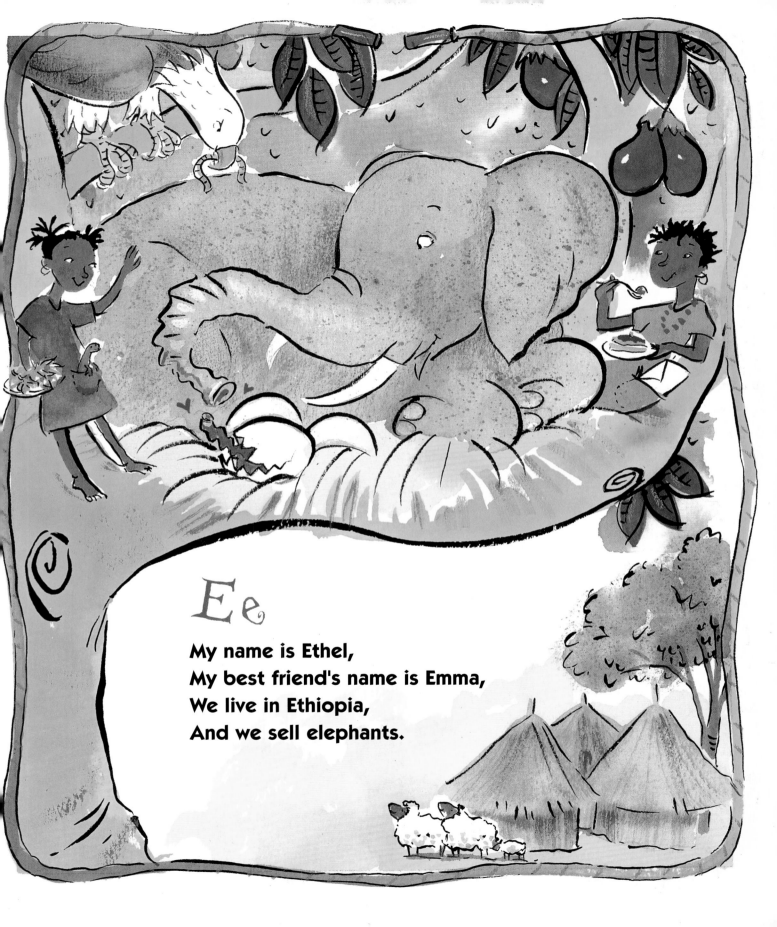

E e

My name is Ethel,
My best friend's name is Emma,
We live in Ethiopia,
And we sell elephants.

My name is Frankie,
My best friend's name is Freda,
We live in Guatemala,
And we sell giants.

H h My name is Hannah,
My best friend's name is Harry,
We live in Honolulu,
And we sell hippos.

My name Ian,
My best friend's name is Ida,
We live in Indonesia,
And we sell iguanas.

My name is Jackson,
My best friend's name is Janice,
We live in Kyoto,
And we sell kittens.

My name is Lisa,
My best friend's name is Lilly,
We live in Louisiana,
And we sell lobsters.

M

m

My name is Maya,
My best friend's name is Mickey,
We live in Minneapolis,
And we sell martians.

Nn
Oo

My name is Nathan,
My best friend's name is Nola,
We live in Ohio,
And we sell oil.

P p

My name is Pedro,
My best friend's name is Pablo,
We live in Puerto Rico,
And we sell parrots.

Qq

My name is Quentin,
My best friend's name is Quincy,
We live in Quebec,
And we sell quail.

My name is Reba,
My best friend's name is Rita,
We live in Sicily,
And we sell salami.

U u

My name is Ursula,
My best friend's name is Uli,
We live in Uruguay,
And we sell umbrellas.

My name is Violet,
My best friend's name is Vinny,
We live in West Virginia,
And we sell waffles.

Very Wonderful Waffles

My name is Xavier,
My best friend's name is Xerxes,
We live in Xanadu,
And we sell xylophones.

My name is Yuri,
My best friend's name is Yoda,
We live in Yugoslavia,
And we sell yo-yo's.

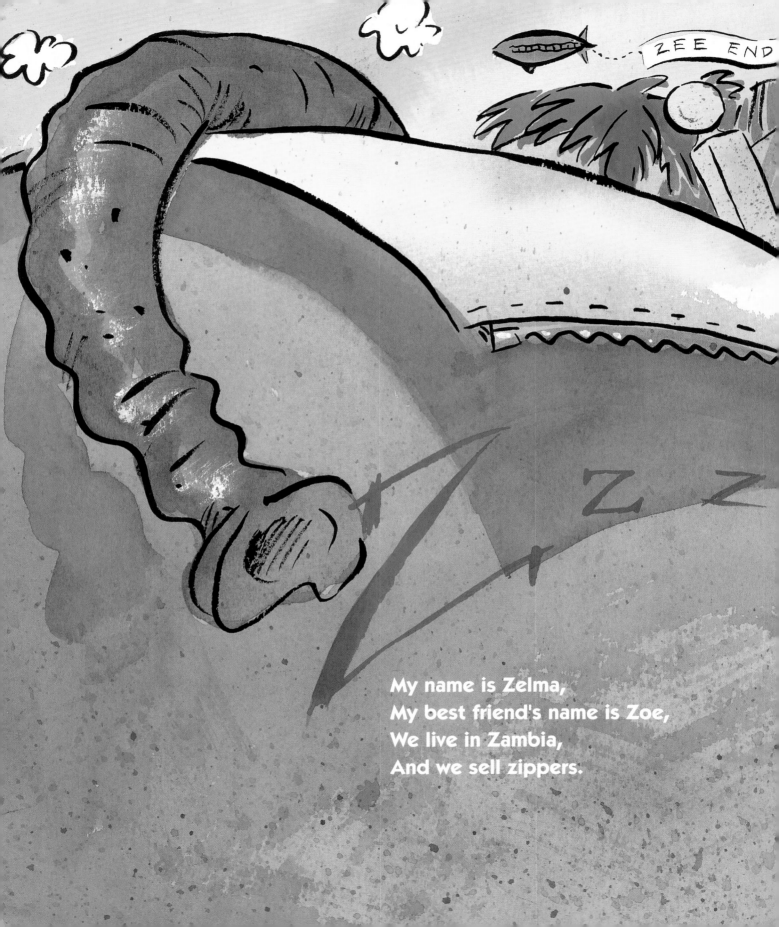

ZEE END

My name is Zelma,
My best friend's name is Zoe,
We live in Zambia,
And we sell zippers.

Can you find these other items in the pictures?

Aa Ace, acorn, afghan, amphibian, anchor, antenna, apricot, avocado, adder, ankle, arm, army of ants, accordion, alligator, apple, arrow.

Bb Cc Bag, balloon, baseball, baseball bat, beads, bumblebee, belt, birds, book, bow, bottle, bracelet, buckle, bug, bush, button, beach, bay, belly button, belly, boy, beach towel, beach ball, bow tie, bikini, bananas, clam, comb, conch, crab, curb, cloud, coast, camera, cat, car, coconut, chauffeur.

Dd Daffodil, daisy, dahlia, desk, dice, dish, doily, door, dove, drapes, dress, drink, doorknob, dog, donkey, diamond, dollar bills, drum, demijohn, decanter, drumsticks.

Ee Ear, eclair, eft, elm, endive, envelope, ewe, eye, eggs, eggplant, earthworm, eagle, earwig, elephant, earrings.

Ff Gg Face mask, feather, foot, feline, fence, fern, fiddle, fingers, fish, fly, food, frog, foxes, flowers, fountain, fruit, garment, garlic, gate, gecko, ground, guava, glasses, goat, giant, grass, grapes, grasshopper, gourd, goose.

Hh Hair, hippos, hand, harbor, head, headdress, hats, harp, hula hoops, hula, hummingbird, hornet.

Ii Iguanas, iceberg, inchworm, ice cream, islands, igloo, ice, infant, insect, iris, ice cube.

Jj Kk Juggling, jam, jump rope, jewelry, jelly beans, jar, jug, jacket, jacks, jeans, jack o'lantern, Japanese, judo, kite, key, kimono, karate, kick, kittens, kiwi, kiss, kid.

Ll Lobster, llama, lizard, lantern, lighthouse, life vest, lake, land, lark, ladder, line, lollipop, loon.

Mm Martian, moon, magazine, mannequin, mat, milk, mirror, moth, mask, mug, mouse, magnet, marbles, money, mummy.

Nn Oo Nest, net, newspaper, nickel, noodle, nose, note, nozzle, oil, oak, oyster, okapi, onion, opossum, orchid, ostrich, ottoman, oil rig.

Pp Paint, pail, palm, pants, parakeet, pear, pebble, pen, pencil, pot, poodle, pretzel, pig, peanuts, pottery.

Qq Queen, quart, quilted hot pads, quince, quail.

Rr Ss Ring, rodent (rat), radio, rose, railing, rooster, scarf, sandals, ship, sandwich, swiss cheese, sea, soda, salad, sailboat, sign, shadow, shrub, slope, smile, stand, stem, straw, salami.

Tt Turtle, tackle, treasure chest, tree trunk, trumpet, T-shirt, teapot, tadpoles, tambourine, tuna, tuba, toes.

Uu Umbrella, unicorns, ukulele, uphill, urchin

Vv Ww Vase, vest, vegetables, vine, visor, valence, wall, witch, wallet, wasp, weasel, wick, wig, wombat, wood, woodchuck, wren, wing, water melon, window, watch, waitress, wood stove, wolves, water, waffles.

Xx Xylophone, xebec.

Yy Yoyos, yellow yarn, yaks, yacht, yawn, yoga.

Zz Zebra, zoo, zipper, zeppelin, zither, Zulus.